R0061950523

07/2012

D1195517

Hip, Hip, Hooray! It's Family Day!

Sign Language for Family

by Dawn Babb Prochovnic
illustrated by Stephanie Bauer

Content Consultant:
Lora Heller, MS, MT-BC, LCAT
and Founding Director of Baby Fingers LLC

magic wagon

For six special grandparents, with love: Grandma Teena and Grandpa Henry;
Nanna and Pee Paw; and Gram B and Pappy—DP
To Mom and Dad....XOXO—SB

Published by Magic Wagon, a division of the ABDO Group, PO Box 398166, Minneapolis, Minnesota 55439.
Copyright © 2012 by Abdo Consulting Group, Inc. International copyrights reserved in all countries. All rights reserved. No part of this book may be reproduced in any form without written permission from the publisher.

Looking Glass Library™ is a trademark and logo of Magic Wagon.

Printed in the United States of America, North Mankato, Minnesota.
102011
012012
 This book contains at least 10% recycled materials.

Written by Dawn Babb Prochovnic
Illustrations by Stephanie Bauer
Edited by Stephanie Hedlund and Rochelle Baltzer
Cover and interior layout and design by Neil Klinepier

Story Time with Signs & Rhymes provides an introduction to ASL vocabulary through stories that are written and structured in English. ASL is a separate language with its own structure. Just as there are personal and regional variations in spoken and written languages, there are similar variations in sign language.

Library of Congress Cataloging-in-Publication Data
Prochovnic, Dawn Babb.
  Hip hip hooray! it's Family Day! : sign language for family / by Dawn Babb Prochovnic ; illustrated by Stephanie Bauer.
     p. cm. -- (Story time with signs & rhymes)
  Summary: In this rhyming story accompanied by sign language diagrams, a child enjoys spending time with various family members, including Mommy and Daddy, Auntie Karen and Grandma Rosie, and Baby Jordon and Cousin Nikki.
  ISBN 978-1-61641-837-3
  1. American Sign Language--Juvenile fiction. 2. Stories in rhyme. 3. Parent and child--Juvenile fiction. 4. Families--Juvenile fiction. [1. Stories in rhyme. 2. Families--Fiction. 3. Sign Language.] I. Bauer, Stephanie, ill. II. Title. III. Title: Hip hip hooray! It is Family Day! IV. Series: Story time with signs & rhymes.
PZ10.4.P76Hi 2012
[E]--dc23   2011027065

Alphabet Handshapes

American Sign Language (ASL) is a visual language that uses handshapes, movements, and facial expressions. Sometimes people spell English words by making the handshape for each letter in the word they want to sign. This is called fingerspelling. The pictures below show the handshapes for each letter in the manual alphabet.

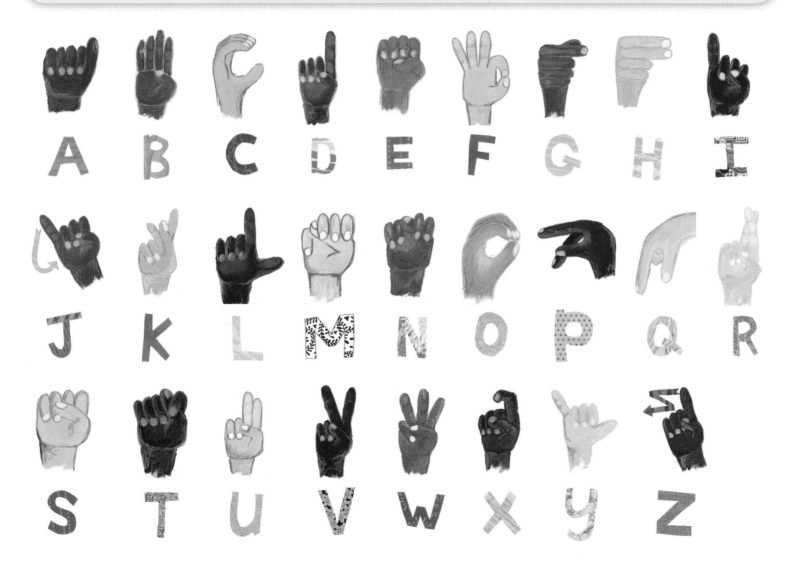

Mommy loves to dance with me.
Whirly, twirly, spin!

mommy

Daddy loves to tickle me.
Wiggly, giggly, grin!

6

daddy

Sister swings so high with me.
Swooshy, whooshy, soar!

sister

Brother runs so fast with me.
Rompy, stompy, score!

brother

Baby Jordon swims with me.
Splishy, sploshy, splash!

baby

Cousin Nikki builds with me.
Wibbly, wobbly, crash!

14

cousin

Auntie Karen rides with me.
Vroomy, zoomy, zoom!

auntie

17

Uncle Charlie drums with me.
Ratty, tatty, boom!

uncle

Grandma Rosie bakes with me.
Roly, poly, pat!

grandma

Grandpa Henry paints with me.
Squooshy, gooshy, splat!

grandpa

Silly **puppy** nuzzles me.
Sloppy, floppy, fur!

24

or

puppy

Fuzzy kitty cuddles me.
Lovey, dovey, purr.

26

kitty

American Sign Language Glossary

auntie: Hold your "A Hand" near your cheek and make a small circle in the air by moving your hand in a forward to back direction.

baby: Hold both of your arms in front of your body and rock them gently back and forth like you are holding a baby.

brother: Sign *boy* by tapping your fingers to your thumb near the top of your head like you are touching the brim of a baseball cap. Then, sign *same* by bringing your pointer fingers in front of you with the sides touching and your palms facing down. This shows your signing partner that you are talking about boys that come from the same family.

cousin: Hold your "C Hand" near the side of your head with your palm facing your cheek and quickly twist the palm of your hand forward and back a couple of times.

daddy: Tap the thumb of your "Five Hand" on your forehead near your eyebrow.

grandma: Touch the thumb of your "Five Hand" to your chin, then move your hand forward by making one or two small arcs in the air.

grandpa: Touch the thumb of your "Five Hand" to your forehead near your eyebrow, then move your hand forward by making one or two small arcs in the air.

kitty: *Use the sign for cat* by moving your "F Hand" from the side of your mouth and out. It should look like you are making cat whiskers. If you want to specify that the cat or kitty is a kitten, you can sign *baby* after signing *cat*.

mommy: Tap the thumb of your "Five Hand" on your chin.

 **or**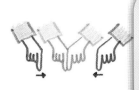

puppy: *Use the sign for dog* by snapping your fingers twice. Another way to sign dog is to pat your hand against the side of your leg a couple of times. It should look like you are calling a dog. If you want to specify that the dog is a puppy, you can sign *baby* after signing *dog*.

sister: Sign *girl* by tracing your jawline from your ear to your chin with the thumb of your "A Hand." Then, sign *same* by bringing your pointer fingers in front of you with the sides touching and your palms facing down. This shows your signing partner that you are talking about girls that come from the same family.

uncle: Hold your "U Hand" near the side of your head and make a small circle in the air by moving your hand in a forward to back direction.

Fun Facts about ASL

Most signs that refer to male family members are signed near the forehead, and most signs that refer to female family members are signed near the mouth or chin. Some say this goes back to the time when only boys wore caps on their head and girls wore bonnets that tied under their chin.

Proper names, such as Jordan or Nikki, are often fingerspelled. A special tradition in the Deaf community is to give individuals a name sign. This is a unique sign that is created by someone in the Deaf community. It can be used in place of fingerspelling to identify an individual by name. It is generally considered disrespectful for people in the hearing community to create name signs for themselves or others.

Some signs use the handshape for the letter the word begins with to make the sign. These are called initialized signs. One example of an initialized sign is the word *uncle*!

Signing Activities

Memory Game: This is a fun game for a classroom or a group of friends to play together. Stand in a circle and choose someone to begin. The first player says, "I'm having a party and I invited my ____" and they make the sign for one family member. The second player repeats the sentence and adds a new sign, so the second player signs two family members. The third player repeats the sentence and adds a new sign, so the third player signs three family members. A player is out and must sit down if they cannot make the string of signs required on their turn. Play continues with the next player wherever the game left off. The last player left standing wins!

Find Your Match: This is a fun game for a classroom or a group of friends to play together. Get some blank index cards. Select one word from the ASL glossary and write that word on the front of two cards. Repeat this process with different glossary words until there are enough cards for each player to receive one card. Select a leader to shuffle the cards and give one to each player. If the number of players is even, the leader will need to keep one card and play the game. If the number of players is odd, the leader will not keep a card. Play begins once the leader says, "Go." The object of the game is for each player to find another player with a matching card, without talking. To accomplish this, each player must make the sign for the word written on their card and search for another player making the same sign. When players with matching cards find each other, they must sit down. Play continues until all players are sitting down.

Additional Resources

Further Reading

Coleman, Rachel. *Once Upon a Time* (Signing Time DVD, Series 2, Volume 11). Two Little Hands Productions, 2008.

Edge, Nellie. *ABC Phonics: Sing, Sign, and Read!* Northlight Communications, 2010.

Heller, Lora. *Sign Language for Kids*. Sterling, 2004.

Valli, Clayton. *The Gallaudet Dictionary of American Sign Language*. Gallaudet University Press, 2005.

Web Sites

To learn more about ASL, visit ABDO Group online at **www.abdopublishing.com**. Web sites about ASL are featured on our Book Links page. These links are routinely monitored and updated to provide the most current information available.